# Favorite Stories from Cowgirl Kate and Cocoa

# Favorite Stories from Cowgirl Kate and Cocoa

Written By **Erica Silverman**

Painted By **Betsy Lewin**

sandpiper

Green Light Readers

Houghton Mifflin Harcourt

Boston   New York

First Green Light Readers edition, 2013

www.hmhbooks.com

The display type was hand lettered by Georgia Deaver.
The text type was set in Filosofia Regular.
The illustrations in this book were done in watercolors
on Strathmore one-ply Bristol paper.


The Library of Congress has cataloged *Cowgirl Kate and Cocoa* as follows:
Silverman, Erica.
Cowgirl Kate and Cocoa/Erica Silverman, illustrated by Betsy Lewin.
p. cm.
ISBN: 978-0-15-202124-5 hardcover
ISBN: 978-0-15-205660-5 paperback
Summary: Cowgirl Kate and her cowhorse, Cocoa, who is always hungry,
count cows, share a story, and help each other fall asleep.
[1. Cowgirls—Fiction. 2. Horses—Fiction.]
I. Lewin, Betsy. Ill. II. Title.
Pz7.S58625Co 2005
[E]—dc22 2004005739

ISBN: 978-0-544-02268-3 paper over board
ISBN: 978-0-544-02267-6 paperback

Manufactured in China
SCP 10 9 8 7 6 5 4 3 2 1

4500400037

To Julio, the newest Torn —E.S.

To horses everywhere —B.L.

# The Surprise

One morning
Cowgirl Kate brought a box
to the barn.

"What is in that box?" Cocoa asked.

"A surprise," said Cowgirl Kate.

"Sugar cookies?" he asked.

"A surprise," she said.

"Apple pie?" he asked.

"A surprise," she said.

"Give me my surprise!" he said.

"First eat your oats," she said.

Cocoa glared at the bucket.

He kicked it over.

Cowgirl Kate frowned.

"That was your breakfast," she said.

Cocoa snorted.

"I am done with my breakfast," he said.

"I want my surprise."

"First I must groom you,"
said Cowgirl Kate.
She curried him.

She brushed him.

Then she cleaned his hooves.

Cocoa stomped.

"I want my surprise now!"

He pushed open the box.

He took a big bite
of the surprise.

He chewed.

He swallowed.

"Yuck!" he said.

"This does not taste
good at all!"

"Of course not," said Kate.

"It is a hat."

She put the hat on Cocoa's head
and held up a mirror.

"Do you like it?" she asked.

Cocoa frowned.

"I have only two ears," he said.

"But this hat has three holes!"

Cowgirl Kate laughed.

"Next time," she said,

"eat your breakfast

and not your surprise."

# Bedtime in the Barn

One night Cowgirl Kate slept in the barn.
"Good night, Cocoa," she said.
She crawled into her sleeping bag
and closed her eyes.

"Will you please fluff my straw?" Cocoa asked.

Cowgirl Kate sighed.

"I am very tired," she said.

But she climbed out of her sleeping bag
and fluffed his straw.
Then she crawled back into her sleeping bag.

"I am hungry," said Cocoa.

Cowgirl Kate sighed.

"You are always hungry," she said.

But she climbed out of her sleeping bag
and gave him three carrots.
Then she crawled back into her sleeping bag.

"Uh-oh! My water bin is low," said Cocoa.

Cowgirl Kate groaned.

"Why didn't you tell me that before?"

"I didn't think of it before," said Cocoa.

"First I was thinking about straw.

Then I was thinking about food.

Now I am thinking about water."

"You are doing too much thinking,"

said Cowgirl Kate.

But she climbed out of her sleeping bag
and filled up his water bin.

"Is there anything else?" she asked.

"No," said Cocoa.

"Good," she said.

"Now think about sleep!"

"Good night, Katie," said Cocoa.
"Good night, Cocoa," said Cowgirl Kate.

The barn was cold.

Cowgirl Kate pulled the sleeping bag up to her chin.

The moon was bright.

She pulled the sleeping bag over her eyes.

An owl hooted outside.

*Whoooooo. Whoooooo.*

Cowgirl Kate shivered.

"Cocoa! I cannot sleep," she said.

"Then I will sing you a lullaby," said Cocoa.

"Rock-a-bye, cowgirl,
on your cowhorse.
Though the wind blows,
you'll never be tossed.
When the dawn breaks,
your cowhorse will say,
'My hat's on. I'm ready
to herd cows all day.'"

And Cowgirl Kate smiled,
snuggled close . . .
and fell asleep.

**Erica Silverman** is the author of a series of books about Cowgirl Kate and Cocoa, the original of which received a Theodor Seuss Geisel Honor. She has also written numerous picture books, including the Halloween favorite *Big Pumpkin*, *Don't Fidget a Feather!*, *On the Morn of Mayfest*, and *Liberty's Voice.* Her new easy reader series, Lana's World, will be available from Green Light Readers soon. She lives in Los Angeles, California.

**Betsy Lewin** is the well-known illustrator of Doreen Cronin's *Duck for President*; *Giggle, Giggle, Quack*; and *Click, Clack, Moo: Cows That Type*, for which she received a Caldecott Honor. She lives in Brooklyn, New York.